STRANGE TALES

DANIEL MORDEN has enthralled audiences with his performances of traditional stories for more than thirty years. He is as comfortable in front of a nursery of small children as he is in a theatre with three hundred adults. His work has taken him all over the world, from remote villages in the Arctic to the National Theatre. He is also the author of many anthologies of traditional stories, and his writing retains the propulsive momentum of a live performance. Though he tells many kinds of story, he is particularly known for telling mysterious fairy tales like the ones contained in this book.

In 2017 he was awarded the Hay Festival Medal for his storytelling. He lives in Abergavenny with his family.

STRANGE TALES

DANIEL MORDEN

Firefly

First published in 2023
by Firefly Press
25 Gabalfa Road, Llandaff North, Cardiff, CF14 2JJ
www.fireflypress.co.uk

A CIP catalogue record of this book is
available from the British Library.

ISBN 978-1-915444-17-2

This book has been published with the support
of the Books Council of Wales.

Typeset by Elaine Sharples

Printed by CPI Group (UK) Ltd, Croydon CR0 4YY

MIX
Paper | Supporting
responsible forestry
FSC® C171272

To Marion

CONTENTS

CONTENTS

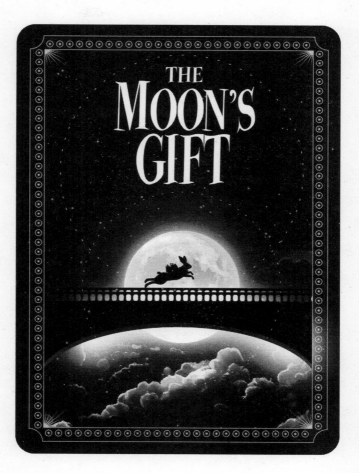

THE MOON'S GIFT

I

 In the beginning the shining king and the glittering queen of the sky were husband and wife. They lived in harmony. Sometimes he rode the heavens in her sledge, sometimes she rode in his chariot. He loved her and she loved him.

The problems came when they had a child. With the child came bitter bickering and sullen silence. The child was the Earth. At first the Earth was lifeless, but then two-legged things appeared: men and women. From the moment she saw them, the Queen of the Moon loved them. She watched them like a parent, with infinite compassion. She wanted only good for them.

They knew nothing. They did not know how to speak or walk or sleep. There was nothing for them to eat, nowhere for them to shelter…

The shining king was jealous of the time the queen spent doting over them.

She said, 'They're helpless. We have so many things that we could give them that would ease their lives...'

'You waste your love on them. They are weak.'

'They will thrive if we help them.'

'As long as they are helpless, they are no threat. If they thrive, don't turn your back on them. They will overrun us. Overthrow us.'

She saw him gathering weapons to use against the people. He had every intention of killing them all.

The shining king and the glittering queen spoke less and less.

One day, while her husband was busy, guiding his blazing chariot across the sky, she gathered the things she needed. She wanted to take them to the Earth, but if she went down there, he would see ... Ah! She would send her servant. That scatterbrained hare.

She gave the hare two boxes: a white box and a red one.

'Take them to the people. I will wait until my husband is asleep then join you. Tell the people they must only open the white box. When I arrive,

I will teach them how to use the things inside. And as for the red one…' she saw the hare had forgotten half her instructions. 'Just take them both boxes. I will explain everything when I arrive.'

The hare set off.

'And, hare—'

'Yes, Your Highness?'

'The boxes are for the people. Not for you. Don't open them.'

In those times there were bridges between Earth and the heavens. As the hare scuttled down a bridge, a million thoughts passed through his scatterbrain.

I wonder what she's giving them.

What harm would there be in knowing?

What is so special about man and woman?

What about me?

Don't I deserve gifts after such devoted service?

The boxes are so light. She probably forgot to put anything inside.

What harm would there be in looking in an empty box? And who will know that I have done so?

So, he lifted the lid of the white box.

He was thrown onto his back. Out came birds

and beasts and bees and seeds. Grain and pollen and fire, and countless good things that the glittering queen knew would help our lives.

Now for the red! Out came disease and madness and jealousy and greed. Snakes and scorpions and pain and death. The things the queen's husband had been gathering to use against Earth. She was sending them to Earth so that the people could hide them from her husband.

When the queen saw what had happened, she tried to retrieve the awful things, but they scuttled into the shadows and wriggled into the crevices.

So she did the best she could. She taught the people how to use the good things she had given them. How to make fire to stay warm and to cook. How to grow crops. How to keep animals.

But the people were terrified of the scuttling, whispering things in the shadows.

The people ascended the bridges, pleading with the queen. 'It is safe up here. Let us come and live with you!'

'You see?' said the shining king. 'They aren't content with everything you gave them. They want to be us!'

And he blasted the bridges into dust.

Ever since then the Sun and the Moon have been apart. He built a palace on one side of the Earth, and she on the other. When she is in the sky, he hides his face. When he is in the sky, sometimes she tries to join him, but he will have nothing to do with her.

But the Moon still loves us. Sometimes she walks the world disguised as an old woman, helping those she meets. Often at night we will see her face gazing down, with all the tender love of a parent. Because she loves us, she gave us one last gift to help us endure the torments and disappointments that escaped from the red box…

Stories.

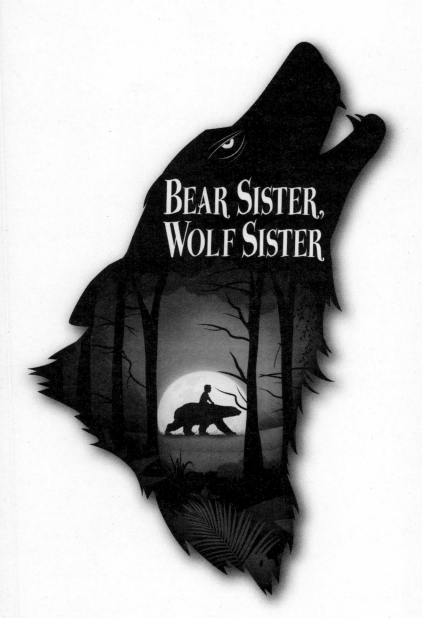

2

Two sisters lived at the foot of a black mountain. One was a farmer – she had sheep and cows – the other a hunter. One day, as the farmer sister watched her herds, a shadow crept down the mountain, enveloped the field and surrounded her. At first, she could see nothing … then she saw something blacker than the shadow. It was the silhouette of a man.

'I am the magician of the black mountain,' he said. 'Marry me, and you will live like a queen.'

'Thank you, but I am happy living like a farmer.'

'Marry me, or I will turn your sheep into stones.'

'I will not!'

Shadow and silhouette vanished. The farmer sister stood in a field of cows … and stones.

A week passed, then the darkness, and its master, returned.

'Marry me and I will give you sapphires.'

'I don't want sapphires; I want sheep.'

'Marry me, or I will turn your cows into rocks.'

'I will not!'

She blinked and found herself in a field of rocks and stones.

When she learned what had happened, the hunter sister said, 'Don't worry, we can live on what I kill.'

But the next morning to their horror, the sisters saw the shadow sliding like smoke under the door of their hut, choking the fire in the grate. The magician appeared.

'Marry me and I will give you diamonds and rubies.'

'I'd rather have sheep and cows!'

'Marry me or I will turn you both into beasts.'

'No. Never!'

The shadow and its master vanished. The sisters' skin became fur, their nails claws, and they fell on all fours.

The farmer was a bear, and her sister a wolf.

Fearful of the swords and the arrows of men, they fled into a forest and hid in a cave.

The days turned to weeks, the weeks into

months. The wolf sister hunted. Every day she returned with a dead animal and laid it at bear sister's feet.

'There. A feast!'

'I can't eat that! I must have berries and roots and nuts!'

'Berries, roots and nuts aren't food. This is food!'

'We are human. Humans don't eat raw meat. Don't you remember?'

The wolf sister said, 'What does it matter who we were? All that matters is who we are!'

'I am still human. If you want to feed me, bring me human food.'

The wolf sister turned and was gone without a word. Later she returned...

'There! Human food.'

'That is a baby!'

'I thought you'd like it! Aren't you going to eat it?'

'I can't.'

'Why not?'

'Because it is us!'

In the days and weeks and months that followed, the bear sister gave the baby milk. The child grew. He was dirty – and happy.

One day, the bear sister said, 'Milk is no longer enough. He needs solid food. Can you get me bread?'

The wolf sister said, 'Bread…'

Far away, the palace was draped in black. Though hunters had been searching day and night, the young prince could not be found. It was as if he had vanished into the air.

One day, a wise man said to the king and queen, 'Your Majesties, there is a certain woman whom it is said is skilled in the secret arts of magic.'

'You mean a witch?' asked the king.

'Some call her a witch, some call her wise. Magic has stolen him, so only magic will find him.'

The king opened his hands. 'Desperate times call for desperate measures. I have heard only good of her. Fetch her!'

'Your Majesty, I should warn you, she … her face…'

When the woman arrived, they saw for themselves. It was hard to look at her. Her skin was fur, her nose a snout and her eyes were like black beads. She bowed.

'Your Highnesses, fetch me something your son wore – and your favourite hound.'

The hound sniffed the shirt. She whispered in the creature's ear. It bounded from the courtyard. The king, the queen and the witch followed it into a forest. They found the spoors and paw prints of wolves and bears.

The king said, 'If some beast has killed our son, its life is forfeit.'

They heard growling. They searched for the source of the sound and found a cave. The king signalled to his huntsmen, who notched arrows to their bows. A bear emerged. The bear saw the king and queen … the king lifted his hand, and his men drew back their bowstrings … but the bear gave the king and queen such a sorrowful look that it wrung their hearts. The bear turned back to the cave and emerged with their son. She placed him carefully before the queen and then lay at the king's feet.

He said, 'This is the strangest beast that ever I saw.'

The witch said, 'That is because she is no beast. She has an animal body but a human soul. She has been cursed by a spell.'

'You! Come with us,' said the king.

The bear looked back at the cave. Warily, a wolf emerged.

The queen wanted to gather her son in her arms, but the boy shrank from her. Instead, he rode to the palace on the bear's broad black back.

'Can you restore these beasts to their true forms?' the queen asked the witch.

The witch sighed. 'How I wish I could! Only the maker can unmake a spell. I will summon the spellcaster.'

She led bear and wolf to a walled garden. The witch lit a fire and whispered words, her eyes on a distant mountain. A shadow appeared on those slopes, but there was no cloud in the sky above to cast it. The shadow engulfed the fields at the mountain's foot, then the forest, then the very garden in which she stood. She fed the flames and whispered more words. Night came, but not a single star. The flames kept the darkness at bay. The air grew thicker and thicker, blacker and blacker, until it was heavy, pressing the witch until she couldn't see, move. She could barely breathe...

Just as she thought the darkness would crush her, there came a shout as was never before heard by woman or man.

The dark dissipated, and there stood the magician.

'I knew this was your doing,' she said.

'You hold no interest for me,' replied the magician. 'Take me to the king and queen.'

Word had spread of the return of the prince, and the mysterious beasts who had accompanied him. Lords and ladies, courtiers and advisors had gathered to see these wonders. The magician bowed before the king and queen.

'Your Majesties, I am delighted that your son has been restored to you,' he said. 'His theft was none of my doing.'

'But what of these creatures?' said the queen. 'We are told they are humans whom you enchanted.'

'You were told this by a mad old hag. These animals belong to me.'

'These are people, and they belong to themselves,' said the witch.

He sneered at her.

'If you want them, you'll have to win them. What say you to this, Your Majesties – a contest of magic between me and this one...' he gestured dismissively at the woman '...which you will judge.'

'We should settle this matter another way,' said the witch.

'Can you hear her fear?' the magician cried.

'I admit I am afraid,' she said. 'Every spell comes at a cost. Every act of magic puts us and others in danger.'

The magician sneered again.

'Bring me a bowl.'

A bowl was brought. He filled it with water then passed his staff over it. The bowl was empty! He gave it to the courtiers. They inspected it, passed it from hand to hand, then gave it back to him. He passed his staff over it in the opposite direction and the water reappeared!

The magician handed the bowl to the witch. She passed her hand over it and again the water vanished. Then she gave the bowl to the crowd just as the magician had done. When it was returned to her, she passed her hand over it in the opposite direction and the bowl was filled with wine. The crowd clapped. The magician scowled.

'Bring me a bird in a cage.'

A cage holding a dove was fetched. He opened the cage, fetched out the bird and passed his staff over it. The dove dropped dead. When the courtiers examined it, it was cold and stiff in their hands, devoid of life, devoid of breath. The magician passed his staff in the opposite direction and the dove came back to life. The court cheered. The magician stepped back.

The witch passed her hand over the dove. It fell stiff. Then she passed her hand in the other direction. The dove twitched, rose up and flew above them, singing. It settled on the table, laid an egg that hatched, and a chick popped out. The crowd gasped and laughed.

The magician was shaking with fury. 'One last feat,' he said. 'But she cannot be privy to the spell I speak.' So the witch was led from the hall to an antechamber.

The magician stood his staff in the centre of the hall, spoke a spell and stepped back. The staff sprouted branches, the branches twigs and the twigs leaves. An apple swelled from the uppermost branch. The courtiers were amazed.

'Fetch the hag,' said the magician.

When she returned, she saw the tree and said, 'No more. Magic is not a game. Free the sisters and we need never speak of this again.'

The magician crowed to the crowd. 'I have won! She can't compete with my miracle!'

The old witch sighed. 'Then just as I left when you cast your spell, so you must leave while I cast mine.'

Once the magician left the room, the witch circled the tree three times, then reached up to the highest branch and picked the apple. As soon as she had done so, her face became a human face. The fur shrank into skin, and her snout a nose.

The tree shrivelled and the branches withered. The leaves disappeared as they fell. The staff clattered to the floor.

She held out the apple. One of the courtiers took it. She nodded to a servant. He opened the door to fetch the magician, stumbled and screamed.

The courtiers crowded around him to see what he had seen. The magician's body lay in a corner of the room – and his head in the opposite corner. The courtier looked at the apple in his hand.

When they went to the garden, the witch, the king and the queen found a young woman and a wolf.

The woman said, 'My sister...'

'I am sorry,' said the wolf. 'To go back to what I was, to never again see and smell and hear the world this way, would be to deny my true nature. Goodbye.'

And she loped into the forest.

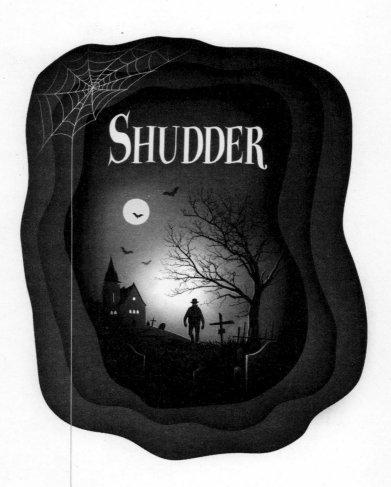

SHUDDER

SHUDDER

3

Once upon a time a farmer had two sons. The first could turn his hand to any task. The second – all he ever did was sit by the fire.

One evening, the farmer handed a letter to his eldest son.

'Take this to your uncle,' he said.

The eldest son shrank back from the letter as though it were a viper.

'But if I go now, I will have to walk past *that* house in the dark! You know the house I speak of, the one they call The House of the Devil. I have heard the stories people tell of the things they have seen inside that house. When I walk past in the daytime I go to the other side of the road and make the sign of the cross as I rush by. To walk past it at night would make me shudder with fear!'

When he heard those words, the younger lad looked up and frowned.

'Shudder…? Fear…?!'

A few weeks later the father called his sons to him and said, 'Soon you will be old enough to make your own way in the world. What trade do you want to learn?'

'I have been thinking,' said the older son. 'I want to learn how to be a farmer, like you.'

'Good!' said the father. Then he turned to the other son. 'And you?'

'I have been thinking too. I want to learn how to shudder with fear.'

'What?'

'Everyone talks about fear, but I don't know what it is. Until I know what fear is, what use will I be to anyone?'

The father rolled his eyes. 'What did I do to deserve you?'

One day, as the father walked past a churchyard, he saw the caretaker raking up the leaves between the gravestones.

'I wonder if you can help me,' he said. 'My youngest son told me he wanted to learn how to shudder. I thought I would send him to the church this evening, and at midnight, when all is still and quiet, you could jump out and teach him what fear is!'

The old caretaker cackled and nodded his head.

The father went home. The younger son was sitting by the fire as usual.

'Hey!' said the father. 'You know the caretaker of the church? He just died. They will bury him in the morning. His body is on a table in the church. I want you to sit by the corpse and keep watch over it until until day comes.'

The lad stood up. Ash billowed from his clothes. Ash tumbled from his pockets.

'My training begins! If I am to spend the night in church, I need something to eat and something to drink. What do they eat in church? Bread! What do they drink? Wine!'

He set off, chomping and swigging. It was night when he reached the churchyard. Mist rose between the gravestones. They leaned together as if sharing secrets. He picked his way between them, chewing and gulping all the while. The church door creaked as he opened it but he didn't notice.

A table had been set in front of the altar. A white

sheet lay over the table. Under the sheet lay the caretaker, pretending to be dead.

I have never seen a dead body before, the lad thought to himself. *Perhaps it will make me shudder with fear.*

He took a gulp of wine, tore off a hunk of bread and began to chew. He lifted the white sheet and peered down at the old man.

The noise of the chewing and the smell of the wine almost ruined the plan. The caretaker was furious! Where were the boy's manners? But he kept up the pretence. He stayed as still as he could and made no sound.

In a minute, he thought, *I will teach him what fear is!*

The lad sat in the front pew, chewing until he'd finished the bread, and swigging until he'd finished the wine. He'd never had wine before. He stumbled around the church, lurching, hiccupping, belching. Under the sheet, the caretaker couldn't believe the lad's impudence!

What kind of a way is this to behave in a church? I won't frighten him; I will give him a piece of my mind!

He threw off the sheet. The lad had his back to

him, swaying back and forth, brandishing the bottle.

'YOU!' said the caretaker. 'Mourners shouldn't be drunk!'

'And the dead shouldn't be alive!' BOK! He hit the old man with the bottle.

Next morning, the lad's father came to see how his son had fared. When he opened the door he saw his son in the front pew – and there, in front of his son, he saw the caretaker's corpse.

'What have you done?!'

'He was supposed to be dead, but he wasn't, so I made him dead!'

'Stop! Don't tell me! I don't want to know. Here!' He threw some coins on the floor. 'Take them. In return, I take back the family name. I am no longer your father, and you are no longer my son. Do what you want, go where you like, only don't come home!'

He stormed from the church.

The lad looked at the coins and looked up.

'It's a deal!' he said. 'Watch out world, here I come! But what will I do? Where will I go? Ah! I know! I will learn how to shudder with fear!'

Every time he met anyone, he asked, 'Excuse me, could you teach me how to shudder with fear?'

Eventually an old travelling woman said, 'Go to Gallows Hill. Spend the night under the corpses and you will learn what fear is!'

'Thank you, my friend! Meet me there tomorrow. If I have learned how to shudder, I'll give you all the coins in my pocket! Which way to Gallows Hill?'

'Take Lonely Road past The Sucking Pit, turn left at The Cave of Doom, through Gloomy Hollow, round Dark Moon Pool, over Grab Ankle Bridge, across Jenny Greenteeth's yard, then you will see them on the gallows tree – the corpses, dancing to the song of the wind!'

'Perfect! See you in the morning!' And off he went.

He waved at the ravens on Lonely Road, lost a shoe in The Sucking Pit, shouted 'Hiya!' into The Cave of Doom, blew raspberries at the beast of Gloomy Hollow, skimmed a stone on Dark Moon Pool, lost the other shoe on Grab Ankle Bridge, petted the growling hound in Jenny Greenteeth's yard and came to Gallows Hill. Crows rose from the branches into the grey sky. The wind stirred the corpses. They twisted on the ropes.

The lad lit a fire. He said to the dead, 'You up there! I am cold sitting next to the fire, so you must be freezing! Come down and join me!'

'No? You are stuck, is that it? I will help you!'

He climbed into the tree and cut the ropes. THUMP! THUMP! THUMP! One by one the corpses fell in a clump. The hangman had left his autograph – bruising on every neck, purple and yellow and crimson. Flies clambered over the corpses' faces. He scrambled down, sat them in a circle, each head on the next one's shoulder.

He shuffled in amongst them and said, 'Anyone know any songs…?'

He sang every song he knew. The rats seemed to enjoy them. The game of charades was less of a success. Next morning the old woman who had sent him to Gallows Hill came to see how he had fared. The lad heard her approach and stood up. The corpses flopped back into the grass.

'Your friends are fools,' he said. 'People say I am foolish, but even I know that when my clothes catch fire, I have to put them out!'

'Well then,' said the old woman. 'If you still don't know how to shudder, there is another place you could try – The House of The Devil. It is infested with all manner of evil things. If anyone can spend one night there without feeling fear, those creatures will have to leave and never return. No man or woman has ever done so. Most of the folk who try, run off screaming at nightfall. Those who stay are driven mad by the dreadful sights they behold. Her Royal Highness, the princess, has offered a great reward to the man or woman who can banish the vile things from that place. Go to her and ask for her permission. If you do feel fear, your dearest wish will have been granted. If you don't, you will have won a great reward!'

'Thank you!' he scooped the coins from his pocket and pressed them into her palm. 'Take these!'

When the guards heard why he had come to the castle, they shook their heads. 'Are you tired of living?'

When the lad insisted, the guards banged their drums and blew their horns and cried, 'Another brave soul wants to take his chances in The House of The Devil!'

The moment he saw the princess and she saw him, it was love. She blushed and said, 'Well! What can I do for *you*?'

'If you please, I want to spend the night in The House of The Devil!'

'I don't want you to. I want you … to stay here … with me!'

'First I must learn how to shudder with fear!'

'If I can't talk you out of it, is there anything you would like to take with you into the house, to keep you … company?'

'Can I have anything?'

She looked him up and down.

'Uh huh…'

'I'll take a chisel!'

'A what?'

'A chisel!'

She rolled her eyes.

'Guards, give him a chisel!'

He put the chisel in his pocket.

In front of The House of The Devil no grass grew, and no birds sang. The leafless trees on either side stretched like veins into the cold sky. The house looked like a head, the windows like eyes, the door a mouth … but the lad didn't notice. He pushed open the door. He found himself in a great hall. Cobwebs stretched from the floor to the ceiling and spiders as big as your hand climbed up the cobwebs into the darkness above. A cavernous fireplace gaped to his left, another to his right. He saw a four-poster bed in one corner and, in the very heart of the hall, a pile of wood that had once been used for a fire. He parted the curtains of cobwebs, lit the wood and waited for something to happen.

At midnight he heard a clatter and a thump. Down the chimney had fallen the top half of a man … the ribs, the arms, the neck and the head. It lay face down in the ash, its skin the colour of the belly of a dead fish. The fingers twitched and gripped the grate. The head lifted and leered at him through a mask of ash. The torso pulled itself out of the fireplace and began to drag itself across the floor, leaving a slug trail behind it. Then he heard another clatter, another thump. A cloud of ash billowed from the other fireplace. Down that chimney had fallen the bottom half – a waist, a pair of legs and feet. The feet pushed the legs and waist out of the fireplace and shuffled across the flagstones toward him.

The boy looked at the one half, then the other, and said, 'Have you met? I have a feeling you two would be great together!'

Now, down the chimneys fell heads and torsos and arms and legs and hands. The hands scuttled like spiders, leaving patterns in the dust. The torsos hopped, the heads rolled, the legs wriggled. The lad watched them gather into a thrashing heap on the other side of the fire, eyes swivelling in their sockets, mouths gulping...

'There are too many heads and too many legs! I have an idea! Bowling!'

He grabbed the legs and arranged them in a triangle like skittles, one at the front, two behind the one, three behind the two, and four behind the three. They tried to resist, but all they could do was bend at the knee. He picked up a head.

'You will be the ball!' He put a finger in each eye

and one up a nostril then bowled. The head never reached the legs. It wobbled and fell in the dust. He picked it up.

'You are the wrong shape! You are knobbly when you are supposed to be round! Don't worry, I have a chisel!'

He drew it from his pocket.

The head looked at the chisel, then the lad, and screamed, 'No!'

'Yes!'

The lad lunged – but there was a flash of light and a puff of smoke and all the bodies and limbs were gone.

Now he saw two lines of candles leading to a table. On the table was a coffin with the lid on. As he walked between the candles they snuffed out. He lifted the lid of the coffin to find an old man in his best suit, his eyes closed and his arms clasped across his chest.

'You must be the father of the house!'

He touched the old man's forehead. It was clammy.

'You are so cold, my friend. Stay there. I will warm you!'

The lad held his hands as close as he could to the

flames of the fire, then pressed them against the old man's cheeks. The skin came off like wet tissue paper.

'Forgive me!'

He carried the body to the bed. He climbed in beside it and rubbed the arms and legs, pulling the sheets over them both.

The bed shook, trembled, lifted from the floor and crashed against a wall. It flew backwards at breakneck speed. It tipped upside down, then bucked like a rodeo bull.

The lad clung on tightly and cried, 'More! Faster!' The bed crashed to the ground. The body beside the lad had changed. The skin was no longer cold, it was warm. Then it was no longer warm, it was hot, burning the lad's hand. The sheets smouldered. He turned to the pillow beside his own, and looking back was the face of the devil. He was in bed with the devil! The devil reared up and gripped the lad's throat, his eyes like blazing coals, his nostrils like trumpets.

The boy cried, 'That's the thanks I get for warming you up?'

The devil stopped. Creatures of the night draw

strength from fear. If you have no fear, they have no strength. The lad grabbed the devil by his beard. He dragged him across the floor, threw him in the coffin, slammed down the lid, sat on the lid and said, 'You are not coming out until you learn how to behave!'

The devil punched the underside of the coffin lid. Gradually the punching became a knocking, the knocking became a scratching, the scratching became a tapping – and then silence. Through the window came the light of the morning. Through the door came the princess.

'Did you learn how to shudder with fear?' she asked.

'No. But guess who is in here!'

He jumped off the coffin, pulled back the lid – and found only dust.

'You have won! The awful things that plagued this place can never return. I promised a great reward to the person who would accomplish this task. As it is you, I will give a great reward indeed … me!'

'I would love to marry you, but I haven't learned how to shudder with fear. Until I know this, what use will I be to you?'

He travelled the world, had many adventures, but never once did he shudder with fear. Eventually he returned to her palace and announced, 'I am incomplete, but my thoughts always return to you, so if you would take me, just as I am, I would gladly be your husband.'

She sent for a priest before he changed his mind.

The priest said, 'Do you take this woman to be your lawfully wedded wife?'

'Priest, could you teach me how to shudder with fear?' asked the lad.

Under her veil, the princess rolled her eyes.

In the years that followed they lived well, but he never stopped yabbering about shuddering with fear. One night the princess was woken by her husband talking in his sleep.

'I just want to shudder with fear!'

Something snapped inside her. She slipped out of bed and pulled a cloak over her shift. She made her way down the stone spiral staircase out into the snow-covered courtyard. It was a bitter night. She threw a rock through the ice on the moat and dipped a bucket into the hole she had made. She made her way back up the stone spiral staircase, pulled back the sheets and tipped the ice-cold water over her husband as he slept.

'Aah!' He reared up.

'Listen to me! I love you, but if I ever again hear you speak of shuddering and fear, I will leave you and you will never see me again! Is that clear?'

An eel wriggled inside his nightshirt. A weed fell from his chin.

'And I love you. Now that I am with you the world is different. I want to spend every waking and sleeping moment with you. I cannot feel anything unless I have shared it with you. If you were to leave, it would be as if my soul had been torn from me. There would be no reason to carry on...' His whole body was trembling. 'This is fear! The thought of you leaving me ... it makes me shudder!'

MISS
FORTUNE

4

There was once a king of Spain. Between him and his wife they had seven daughters. They lived happily, until their eldest daughter had grown as tall as she was going to grow. Then a neighbouring king came with a great army. The King of Spain and his people fought valiantly, but they were defeated; he was taken captive, and the queen and her daughters fled to a distant village, where they had to live in a hovel. They tried to earn a little money by sewing and weaving. Though their work was faultless, nobody seemed to want it, and very often the queen and the princesses had nothing to eat. Sometimes the queen even begged.

One summer evening the daughters were searching the woods for strawberries, and the queen was making a thin broth for their supper, when an old travelling woman came knocking at the door, selling scraps of lace.

'Well, I can give you a bowl of broth,' the queen told her, 'but I have no money. I am the Queen of Spain, whose husband was taken prisoner, and now I and my seven daughters live here in poverty. Come in, rest yourself, and if what little I can offer will satisfy you, you are welcome to it.'

The old woman thanked her and sat by the fire. She drank her bowl of broth, stared into the flames and muttered.

At last she said, 'Your Highness, I have been given the power to look into the past and the future, and to see the causes of things: of the good and evil fortunes that attend us mortals, of the bringing of the one, and the curing of the other. Would you have me tell you the cause of all your troubles? But I should warn you, you will not like what you hear.'

'It is always better to know.'

'One of your daughters is unfortunate. She is cursed with a bitter fate; it is due to her that all this misery has befallen you. Send her away, and everything will be restored to you. Your husband, your nation...'

'How can I abandon one of my children?'

'Is her future worth more than the futures of your other daughters? And your husband? And your people?'

The queen was silent for a while and then she said, 'What does it matter? I don't know which of my daughters is cursed.'

'Wait until your daughters are asleep,' said the old woman. 'Take a candle into their bedchamber and you will know.'

The old woman went on her way, leaving the queen in a state of great distress.

The seven princesses returned.

'We didn't find a single strawberry. It was as if someone had stripped the bushes just this morning. Why does everything go wrong for us?'

'Never mind,' said the queen. 'Perhaps we will have good luck tomorrow.'

'Tomorrow never comes.'

They drank their broth in silence, and then went to bed. The queen sat for a long time by the fire. Then she lit a candle and went into the room where the seven princesses lay together in one rickety bed.

The three on the right lay on their right side,

with their hands tucked under their chins; the three on the left lay on their left side with their hands tucked under their chins. In the middle of the bed the youngest lay on her back, her arms crossed over her breast.

The queen wept. Her tears fell onto the youngest daughter. The child opened her eyes.

'Mother, why do you weep?'

'Have I not cause?'

'If it is because we live in poverty and good fortune never comes to us, you would have wept before tonight, but you have been cheerful and hopeful every day until now. So something happened while we were out. You always tell us to share our worries with you. Perhaps it is time for you to do the same.'

The princess would not accept 'no'; she wheedled the truth from her mother. When the queen had finished her story, her daughter threw her arms around her mother's neck and kissed her.

'Say a prayer and go to sleep. The morning is wiser than the evening.'

The queen went to bed. No sooner was she

sleeping than the princess dressed herself and crept into the night.

She walked until dawn. A house emerged from the gloom. She glanced through the window and saw three sisters working, one at a loom, one spinning and one making lace. She knocked. The woman weaving put down her shuttle and opened the door.

'Do you need a servant?' asked the princess.

The woman looked her up and down.

'What is your name? Miss...'

'Fortune.'

'Well, come in, Miss Fortune. If you work well, then you will find us easy to please.'

The women set her to work, sweeping, cleaning, cooking. She worked with a will, and for a week all went well.

One day one of the women said, 'My sisters and I are going to sell our wares at market. We will be back tomorrow. Lock the front and back door after we have gone. Admit no one until we come back.'

'Yes, mistress.'

The women set off. The princess spent the day cleaning and tidying in preparation for their return. When night came, she went to bed, thinking how pleased the sisters would be when they saw what she had done.

At midnight she was woken by strange sounds from the room below. She slipped out of bed, lit a candle and crept downstairs. In the workroom she saw an old woman, her clothes filthy and torn, her spit flying in rage from her lips as she smashed the loom, the spinning wheel, the chairs, tearing the tapestries from the walls. Then Slobberchops saw her.

'Miss Fortune! Where you go, I will follow. And I will bring with me misery and destruction!'

The princess lunged at her, but Slobberchops blew out her candle. When the princess lit it again, she was alone. How had the woman escaped? Through the locked door? The barred window?

The princess set to work, but there wasn't enough time to repair the damage the old woman had done. Next morning, the sisters returned.

'This is what we get for taking you in and trusting you! Be off with you, you ungrateful wretch!' said the oldest sister.

They threw her out. She walked and walked, following the road wherever it took her.

When the shadows began to stretch, she came to a village.

'You, there!' called a woman in an apron standing outside a baker's shop. 'Are you hungry?'

The princess nodded.

'Come in! It would be a sad world if people like me wouldn't spare a bite to eat for someone like you!'

The shop was crammed with good things – baskets of cakes and bread and cheese and fruit and vegetables.

'You can choose anything,' the baker said. 'The day is done. Anything you don't eat I will throw away. I will be baking again in the morning.' The princess ate much and said little.

'Where are you going? Have you somewhere to sleep tonight?'

She shook her head.

'Soon it will be dark. The roads at night are not for one such as you. You can sleep at the back of the shop if you want. At least there you will be safe, and warm from the oven. '

The princess thanked her. The baker made a nest for her amidst the sacks of flour.

Soon the princess was asleep, her hands crossed over her breast.

At midnight something woke her. She lit a candle – and saw Slobberchops! The princess watched her rip the cakes to crumbs, tip the baskets of fruit and vegetables and stamp on them until the floor was covered in a sticky mush. Then she pulled the bungs from the caskets, so the room was flooded with wine and beer.

'Did you think you could escape your fate? Where you go, I follow. You can no more rid yourself of me than you can of your shadow!'

Next morning, the baker was furious!

'Look what you have done!' she said. She pushed Miss Fortune out of the door.

The poor princess fled from the village. She ran so far that she left her father's old kingdom behind. For three years she suffered at the hands of her bitter fate. Wherever she went she was shown kindness, but every act of kindness was punished. Slobberchops pursued her, spitting and shrieking like one of the Furies. Many a night she wept herself to sleep.

One morning as she lay in a forest she was

awoken by the rising sun. She opened her eyes and looked about her. How thirsty she was! She heard the babbling of a brook. As she approached it, she saw a travelling woman washing clothes in the water. When the travelling woman saw the princess, she gave a gasp.

'I know you! You are Miss Fortune!'

'Yes, and if you know what is good for you, you will stay well away from me.'

'But it is because of me that you are all alone in the world. I was the one who told your mother your secret.'

'I am glad that you did. I would rather suffer alone than make misery for my family and the people of my land. But how did you know of my fate?'

'We travelling people know secrets hidden from you and yours. Listen to me now! When a mortal is born, they are given a companion – a spirit that accompanies them throughout their lives. This companion is called a fate. My fate is kind. Though I am not rich, mine is a happy life. Your fate is cruel, so although you were born with every privilege, you suffer every misery.'

'What can I do?'

'That I don't know, but you could ask my fate. I will tell you where to find her.'

The travelling woman gave Miss Fortune a jar of honey. The princess scrambled up the side of a rocky hill until she found a buzzing cave. Inside the cave was a figure lying on the ground as if asleep, covered in bees. The princess took the lid from the jar. The bees flew to the honey, revealing a woman. She opened her eyes and sat up.

'The travelling woman thanks you for the happiness you have granted her,' the princess said. 'She asks if you would do me a great kindness and tell me where I will find *my* fate?'

'Climb to the ridge,' the fate of the travelling woman replied. 'Take the track through the thicket. In the middle of that thicket you will find her, sitting under a thorn bush beside a pool. Take these.' And she gave the princess a dress, a sponge, a bar of sweet-smelling soap, a towel, a hairbrush and a comb.

'This is what you must do…'

The princess scrambled to the top of the hill. She saw the path leading through the thicket. There she found her fate squatting under a thorn bush next to a pool.

'You!' said her fate. 'Get out of my sight! I hate you above all living things!'

But the princess grabbed her fate and threw her into the pool. She tore off her fate's ragged clothes. She washed her from head to foot with sponge and soap, singing as she did so. At first her fate screamed and fought, but as the dirt came from her skin the screaming and fighting subsided. The princess, still singing, lifted her out of the pool and dried her with the towel. Her fate was no longer a cruel old woman. She was neither old nor young. She was ageless – and to the princess she was beautiful. The princess teased all the tangles from her white hair and presented her with the dress. Her fate accepted it. She put it on and smiled.

'My fate, in return for my service to you, I ask a favour. Give me a new name.'

'From this moment you will be Felicia. Take this in return for the dress...'

And she gave the princess a little box. Felicia thanked her fate and scrambled down the slope back to the travelling woman.

Once she had told her friend everything that

had transpired, they heard horses approaching. It was two soldiers.

'Come with us!'

They were taken to the palace of that country and ushered into the private chambers of the young king himself.

'Might you be the travelling woman who is famed for her powers of divination?' he asked.

'Your Majesty, I am the very same.'

'It is fate that my guards chanced upon you! I need your help. Tomorrow is the trooping of the colour. I must inspect the army before my entire nation. This morning I checked my uniform to discover...' He pointed at his jacket. One button was missing.

'I have sent servants to scour the markets and shops of the city, and no one, not even the finest merchant, has the button I seek! What should I do?'

'Your Majesty, in my experience, if you do not draw attention to your flaws, no one notices them.'

'*I* will notice! Do you think it is easy to stand before thousands? This isn't a uniform, it is armour. It protects me, so that I can endure the gaze of so many eyes. Without that button I might as well be naked! What on earth am I to do?'

Felicia held up the box. He lifted the lid and gasped. Inside was the exact button that he needed.

The king bowed and said, 'I thank you from the bottom of my heart! As a sign of my deep gratitude, I will pay for this box with its weight in gold! Guards! Fetch a pair of scales!'

Once the weighing scales had been fetched, in one pan the king put the box with the button and into the other a gold coin. The box was heavier, so he put on a second coin. Still the box outweighed the gold. Another coin, and another...

Eventually he tried a bag ... then a sack ... a second sack, a third...

He looked at the princess and asked, 'Who are you? What is your name?'

'My name is Felicia.'

'Well then, Felicia, where did you get this box?'

She told her story. When she had finished, the king sent for the spinner, the weaver, the lacemaker, the baker, and everyone who had shown her kindness during those three dreadful years. He gave them gold enough to repay the damage wreaked by Felicia's unhappy fate. When he had finished, he said, 'As for your father, the King of Spain was freed from his prison three years ago. He and your mother and sisters have lived in the palace ever since. They will be wondering where you are and if you are safe. I will send word.'

Felicia lived in the palace with her friend, the travelling woman, until one day the woman said, 'I grow tired of staring at the same four walls. What care I for a bed with a velvet canopy when I can sleep beneath a canopy of stars? What care I for the music of minstrels when I can hear the songs of birds? What care I for fine wine when I could drink sweet water from a mountain stream?'

Felicia thanked her, wished her farewell, and the travelling woman walked on, into another story.

After some time, a carriage arrived at the palace.

A messenger came to Felicia's room.

'Your mother, the Queen of Spain, is here,' he said.

Her mother had aged. She wept when she saw her daughter.

'As soon as you left, our good fortune returned,' she said. 'Once again, we rule in the palace, but now we have known hardship, we rule with greater kindness. From the moment that you left I have grieved your absence. I have searched the world to find you. Forgive me my daughter.'

Felicia said, 'There is nothing to forgive. You did not throw me out. It was my choice to leave you, and if I had not fled you would still be begging, and I would not have found and changed my fate.'

Mother and the daughter embraced, and both kingdoms, ruled with kindness, flourished in peace for many a long year.

THE
LUCK
CHILD

Once upon a time a baby was born by the sea in a hut made of the broken bits of boats. The baby's mother and father had nothing: they lived on what the ocean gave them. But they had a friend, an old woman in a nearby village who delivered children, so the child came into the world safely.

On the child's forehead she saw a birthmark. She shook her head in wonder.

'I know by this mark that one day your son will marry a princess,' she said. 'This is a Luck Child!'

That was big news. The old woman returned to where she lived and told her neighbours. The neighbours told the people of the village. The people of the village had to go to the town on market day. They told the tale in the town. The people in the town told the people in the city. In the city there was a castle, so the news reached the ears of the king. When he heard that his beautiful daughter, who'd just been born, was destined to marry a boy who lived in a hut made of the broken bits of boats, he thought, *I won't let that happen. Before my daughter is old enough to lay eyes on this boy, I'll kill him.*

The king dressed himself in a disguise and crept out of the palace in the middle of the night. He searched the coast of his kingdom until he found a hut on a beach, a hut made of the broken bits of boats. He went to the door and knocked. The door was opened by the baby's father. There stood a stranger who said, 'I was passing by when I heard your baby crying. Girl or boy?'

'We have a boy.'

'A boy ... do you know how lucky you are? I am rich, but you are the ones who are lucky. You have a child! My wife is dead; I'll never marry again. As I passed by and heard your baby, I thought, What hope has the child here? Living in a hut made of the broken bits of boats. I know it will be hard for you, but if you love your son, you'll give him to me. I can take him to the city and give him every privilege. And, with my help, who knows, he may even marry a princess!'

The baby's father looked at the baby's mother.

'It is fate that you have come to the house this day. We are meant to give our child to you. You are how he comes to marry the princess.' Their eyes filled with tears; they handed the child to the stranger.

'You will take care of him?'

'Don't you worry; I'll take care of him!'

The king rode off with the baby to the nearest river and threw it in. The child was swept out of sight.

'That is the last I will ever see of him!'

Fifteen years passed. The king was riding through a forest when it began to rain. He saw a mill and he decided to take shelter. He tied up his horse, went to the door and knocked. It was opened by a boy about fifteen years old. The king hung up his cloak and stood by the fire, dripping and steaming. The miller and his wife joined them.

The king said, 'Miller, answer me honestly, is that your son? He is tall and fair and handsome, whereas you are short and dark and ... hairy.'

'How strange you should ask that question today, Your Highness!' said the miller. 'Fifteen years ago to this day, my wife and I went to church to pray for a child. As we walked home beside the river, we saw that God had granted our wish in the most unexpected way. There, floating on the surface of the water, was a baby. So, we brought him up as though he were our own flesh and blood. And there he is, all grown!' The boy blushed and bowed his head. When he did, the king saw that birthmark!

'What a lovely story,' the king said. But he thought, *It's that boy again! I tried to kill him once and failed. I'll try a second time.*

'Boy, I need you to do me a favour,' he said out loud. 'Fetch me something to write with.'

The king wrote a note. 'There now, I need you to carry this message to the queen in the city. Take my horse, he knows the way.' The boy put the note in his pocket, jumped on the king's horse and off he went.

The note read, 'Dear Queen, As soon as this boy arrives, cut off his head! Signed, the King.'

The boy had never ridden a horse before: the miller only had a donkey. Horses are faster than donkeys. As the horse galloped through a forest, there was a low branch, and – CRACK! – suddenly the boy was lying on his back in the middle of the road. He sat up and found that he had a lump the size of an egg on this forehead.

'I can't go any further now, my head is spinning. Ah, I see a strange cottage in the middle of a dark forest. What better place to sleep?'

He went to the door and knocked. Like all the best doors in all the best stories, as the door swung open it creaked. There was an old woman. Her nose went down, her chin came up and they nearly met in the middle. Her long white hair clung to itself like rats' tails.

'I wonder if you can help me,' the boy said. 'I've bumped my head and need somewhere to rest. As a matter of fact, I am on an important errand. I've got a letter in my pocket, written by the king for the queen! Anyway, can I sleep here tonight?'

'If I lived alone, you'd be welcome, but I am the cook for a band of thieves and murderers. If they find you here when they return, they'll give your neck a smile!'

'What do you mean?'

'They will cut your throat!'

'Why?'

'Because they are evil!'

'What is evil?'

She shook her head in disbelief.

'You need my help! Come inside!' She pointed. 'Lie down on that straw. I'll put some more straw on top of you and a blanket on top of the straw. They'll never know you're here.'

As soon as she covered him in the blanket and the straw, he fell asleep. Later, in came the cut-throats. One of them pointed at the pile.

'What is that?'

'It's just a pile of straw.'

'Then why is it snoring?'

'There's a boy in the straw, but he won't harm you. He didn't even know what evil was. As a matter of fact, he is on an important errand. He has a note written by the king for the queen.'

The cut-throats looked at each other.

'Are you thinking what I'm thinking?' one said.

'I'm thinking that I *am* thinking what you're thinking,' said another. 'Let's read the note. Maybe it will tell us who he is. He might be worth something alive. Maybe we could kidnap him and charge a ransom.'

Times were hard. They had had to diversify. They weren't just thieves and murderers; they were also pickpockets. They crept to where the boy was sleeping and drew the note from his pocket. They passed it between them. 'This boy is carrying the order of his own murder! The king wants this boy dead. The king wants us dead. Our enemy's enemy is our friend. We should help him!'

Times were very hard. They weren't just cut-throats, murderers and pickpockets, they were also forgers. 'I know,' said one of the cut-throats. 'We'll copy the king's handwriting and write another note, throw the real one in the fire and put the forgery in its place!'

'What shall we write on the new note? Aha! They wrote – 'Dear Queen, As soon as this boy arrives, have him married to our daughter. Signed, love and kisses, the King.'

The boy woke up next morning with no inkling of what the thieves had done. They had made themselves scarce. He thanked the old woman, jumped on the king's horse and off he went.

Meanwhile, the king waited for a few days at the mill.

'Whichever way the boy went, he's dead by now,' he said to himself. 'I'll go back to the castle.'

Then he realised. 'Oh! I gave that boy my horse… Miller! I need your donkey.'

It was most embarrassing to travel on a donkey. Finally, he reached the city. On every flagpole of his castle, he saw a flapping flag.

That's funny, he thought. *They only put flags out when there's been a…!*

He heard music and dancing. *That's odd. They only have music when there has been a…!*

The air was full of delicious aromas. Had they had a feast? Like after a…

When he reached the gates, he was met by a guard.

'Your Highness, we obeyed your order. As soon as he arrived, we had that lad married to your—'

'WHAT!'

The king ran into the courtyard – confetti everywhere! Music, laughter, dancing … there was his daughter in a wedding dress, and in her eyes there was love.

What am I going to do now? thought the king. *If I kill him, it will break my daughter's heart! I know, I'll send him on a mission, a quest, from which he will never return.*

He smiled at the boy. 'There's just one more thing you must do before you can live with my daughter happily ever after.'

'Your Highness, after allowing me to marry your daughter, I'll do anything.'

'Anything?'

'Anything!'

'Did everyone hear him say he'd do anything? Good! Then go to hell and fetch three golden hairs from the head of the devil.'

The musicians fell silent.

The dancers stopped dancing.

'I beg your pardon?' said the queen.

'Daddy, what did you say?' asked the princess.

'Whah…?' said the boy.

The king said, 'I want three golden hairs from the head of the devil. The sooner you leave, the sooner you'll return. Off you go!'

The boy climbed onto a horse. He looked down at the princess sadly and said, 'I will return!'

And he –
Rode for a day
And he rode for a week,
And he rode for a month,
And rode for a year
And he rode for a year and a day…

…until he came to a city in a desert. The guards saw him approach and shouted, 'Hey! Who are you and what do you know?'

'I am a fool and I know nothing!'

'A fool who knows he is a fool is a rare thing. Help us! In our city there is fountain. The fountain gave us our water. The fountain has stopped flowing. Can you tell us why?'

'I can't tell you why, but I'm going to hell. I'll find the answer, and when I do, I'll come back and tell you.'

And he –
Rode for a day
And he rode for a week,
And he rode for a month,
And rode for a year
And he rode for a year and a day...

...until he came to a city on a mountain.

The guards said, 'Hey! Who are you and what do you know?'

'I am a fool and I know nothing!'

'A fool who knows he is a fool is a rare thing. Help us! In our city there was an apple tree that gave golden apples, but the tree is dying. Can you tell us why?'

'I can't tell you why, but I'm going to hell. I'll find the answer and when I do, I'll come back and tell you.'

And he –
Rode for a day
And he rode for a week,
And he rode for a month,
And rode for a year
And he rode for a year and a day…

…until he came to the end of the world. Everything was grey: grey sky; grey sea; rain, rain, rain. An ancient man sat shivering in a boat. His arms and legs were as thin as twigs. Every time the wind blew, he shuddered.

He said, 'Do you want to cross?'

'Is hell on the other side?'

'This is the ferry to hell. I am the ferryman. Get in!'

So, the boy got in.

The old man said, 'Who are you and what do you know?'

'I am a fool and I know nothing!'

'A fool who knows he is a fool? You're the first one I ever met. Help me. I can't die. My hands are stuck to these oars. Two thousand years – more – I've been rowing this boat. Every day I grow weaker and suffer more pain. I had a wife and daughter long ago. They're in Heaven waiting for me, but I can't die while my hands are stuck to these oars. How can I be free?'

'I don't know, but I'm going to hell. I'll find the answer and when I do, I'll come back and tell you.'

'In all the years I've been rowing this boat, no one has ever come back.'

When they reached the other side, they saw a beach. At the back of the beach there was a great black wall, so tall you couldn't see the top, so long you couldn't see the ends. The boy saw a black door and knocked. Like all the best doors in all the best stories, as it swung open, it creaked. He felt the heat of the flames against his face, flames so bright he had to shut his eyes, but even with his eyes shut he could see through his eyelids the silhouette of the person who'd opened the door... There – standing in front of the flames of hell – was the devil's granny! Her nose went down, her chin went up and they nearly met in the middle. Her long white hair clung to itself like rats' tails.

'What are you doing here? This is no place for you.'

'I've been sent by my father-in-law. I have to pull three golden hairs from the head of your grandson. Also, I need the answer to three problems I met on my journey.'

And he told her about the city in the desert, the city on the mountain and the old man.

'I don't know the answer to these problems, but the devil will. He makes all the problems in the world. When he returns, I'll trick him into telling me the answers. You hide and leave this to me.'

The boy hid. Soon he heard the door of hell swing open and slam shut. In came a big red nose, a big red chin, eyes blazing like coals.

'What a day!' said the devil.

'Oh, have you had a bad day?' said the devil's granny.

'Bad? Bad? It's been hell!'

'I tell you what, I'll sit here, put your head on my lap and I'll run my fingers through your hair and sing you a lullaby.'

'Would you do that for me? That sounds lovely!'

So, she sat on a chair and the devil sat on the floor in front of her. She ran her fingers through his hair and sang to him. As she did so she found a golden strand. She took it between her finger and thumb and tugged.

'Ow!' he jumped up. 'You just pulled out one of my hairs!'

'I'm sorry. I had a dream. It was so horrid I jumped, and I must have pulled out one of your hairs!'

'What dream would be so terrible it would wake you up?'

'I dreamed I was crossing a desert. I was so thirsty! I came to a city that should have had a fountain, but it had stopped flowing and no one knew why.'

'You dreamed of a place that really exists, far away from here. It is my fault that the fountain stopped flowing. If only the people knew that under the city there is a river in a cave. That river feeds the fountain. I rolled a boulder into the river to block its flow. All they have to do is move the stone, but...'

You know that,
I know that,
they don't know that!
I'm going back to sleep.'

She sang him into slumber again. She found a second golden strand and pulled.

'Ow! You did it again!'

'I had another dream.'

'What was the dream about?'

'An apple tree.'

'Ah! You dreamed of a place far away from here. All the people of the city need to do is wait until midnight. If they were to do so, they'd see a rat come out from under the tree. I sent the rat to eat the roots. If a tree has no roots, a tree gets no water. If a tree gets no water, a tree dies. But…

You know that,
I know that,
they don't know that!
I'm going back to sleep.'

She sang to him again, found the last hair and tugged.

'Ow! What was the dream about this time?'

'I was crossing an ocean…'

'Ah. All that old man needs to do is give someone else the oars. As soon as he puts the oars in another person's hands they will be stuck, and he will be free. Free to die! But…

You know that,

I know that,

he doesn't know that!

I'm going back to sleep.' He drifted off.

The boy stood up from where he had been hiding and listening. He took the three hairs from the devil's granny, mouthed a *thank you* to her, opened the door a crack so it wouldn't creak, walked down the beach and there was the old man.

'You've returned! No one has ever come back before. Did you find out how I can be free?'

'I did. When we get to the other side, I'll tell you how.'

When they reached the shore, once he was a safe distance away, the boy shouted.

'Give someone else the oars, then they'll be stuck, and you'll be free – to die.'

'Soon I'll see my wife and daughter again,' said the ferryman joyfully. 'Thank you! Over the top of the hill there is a donkey heaped with sacks of gold. Take them as my gift to you.'

The boy rode over the top of the hill, tied the donkey behind his horse, and he…

Rode for a day
And he rode for a week,
And he rode for a month,
And rode for a year
And he rode for a year and a day.

He came to the city on a mountain. He told them to wait until midnight and out from among the roots of the tree came a rat. They put it in a sack, threw it in the river and it floated downstream to another story. The people of that city were so pleased with the boy that they gave him a donkey piled high with sacks of gold. He thanked them very much, tied the second donkey behind his horse too, and he…

Rode for a day
And he rode for a week,
And he rode for a month,
And rode for a year
And he rode for a year and a day.

He came to the city in the desert. He told them to search. They found a cave. They followed it deep into the earth until they found a boulder. They rolled it away and a gush of water swept them off their feet. Up above, the fountain flowed again. The people of that city were so grateful that they gave him a donkey piled with sacks of gold. He tied the donkey behind the other two. He thanked them very much. And for the very last time he…

Rode for a day
And he rode for a week,
And he rode for a month,
And rode for a year
And he rode for a year and a day.

At last, he came to the city of his true love. He rode up the hill to the castle, through the gates and saw everyone gathered in the courtyard: the king, the queen and the princess.

'Here, Your Highness, are three golden hairs from the head of the devil!' he said.

The king stared. 'Oh … very good,' he said. 'What is in the sacks on the backs of your donkeys?'

'Gold! I crossed the sea at the very end of the world and there was an island heaped with gold. I filled up all the sacks I had and came back. There is plenty more.'

'What? Gold at the end of the world? Guards! Bring me my horse!'

Off went the king, past the first city, past the second city until he came to the end of the world.

There was an old man sitting in a boat.

'Here, take these!' he said to the king. The king took the oars.

'Help! I'm stuck!' he shouted.

'And I am free…' said the ferryman.

The old man stepped out of the boat. With a sigh he crumbled to dust, but his soul rose up to Heaven. And inside the pearly gates were his wife and daughter. At last, he'd arrived. They opened the gates and opened their arms. The three of them cried tears of joy.

The king is still rowing the boat even now.

The boy married the princess all over again just for fun. There was music, dancing, laughter, and they all lived happily ever after ... apart from the king.

THE
OTHER
EYE

There is a certain hill pocked with caves. It is called the Bryn. The grass grows thick and rank around it. It is said that anyone who goes within five paces of it is lost. Animals avoid it. Once, a fox, with a host of hunting hounds at his tail, approached it, then bristled and threw himself into the pack, as if being torn apart while alive was preferable to whatever waited inside the hill. The hounds wouldn't touch him because the scent of the Bryn was on his coat.

A farming family lived nearby – the Pritchards. Matthew and Mari were happy together. They had three children, the youngest newly born. The only source of argument between them was that she thought chapel was a bore. She only went to please her husband.

One Sunday their baby had a cough, so Mari said she would take the child to the widow Rhys.

Matthew was unhappy about this, for several reasons. First, it meant his wife would miss chapel, and second, the widow Rhys was liked in the village – she had delivered all of their children – but she was also feared. She was an old woman who lived by herself in a cottage full of herbs and charms, so there was gossip.

But Matthew could see Mari's mind was made up. He went to chapel with the two children while his wife went to the widow Rhys with the baby.

A couple of days later, Matthew was working in the yard when he heard Mari scream. He dropped what he was doing and ran into the kitchen to find her stretched out on the floor. Her eyes were open, but she didn't see him. She flinched at something he couldn't see. He looked about. In the doorway, a fat black cat sat with its back to him. It turned lazily and to his horror he saw it had the face of a man. He gasped. The cat bolted.

He lifted up his wife and carried her to the bed. He tried to revive her, but it was as if she was in a trance. As the days turned to weeks, her skin turned sallow. Her yellow sweat stained the sheets.

Of course he sent for what passed for doctors in those days, but they were at a loss.

Each week, Mari aged a year. Swirls and mottles appeared on her skin. Her fingers became bony as twigs, her eyes white as milk.

One day there was a knock at his door. It was the widow Rhys.

'I have news of your wife. I spoke to her last night.'

'How can you have done so? I was with her all night.'

'*That thing* in your bed is not your wife. The Tylwyth Teg have Mari. That is something they have left in her place.'

'Don't come here with your nonsense about fairies! I – I am a good Christian man!'

'Mark my words. *That* will be dead within the month, but Mari still lives!'

The widow turned and was gone.

Within the month Matthew was at the churchyard, beside his wife's grave, surrounded by the people of the village, watching a coffin descend into the ground and the earth shovelled on top.

At such a time, we grasp at straws. We look for

reasons why we have suffered such misfortune. Time and again his mind would return to the cat he saw in the doorway, the cat with the face of a man. And so, much to his surprise, he found himself one day approaching the door of the widow Rhys.

She led him down to the edge of the river where the rushing water meant their voices wouldn't carry. She said, 'You know I'm known as a midwife. Men call at all hours to fetch me to help their wives. One night a fine gentleman came. He led me into the night and lifted me onto his stallion. The moment he shook the reins, the world was a blur, and all the breath was gone from my body. I had no idea which way we went.

'We came to a mansion with many windows. We went inside. A servant led us through halls and chambers. There were fine paintings on the walls and rugs on the floor. We came to a bedroom. There was the lady of the house, and she was in labour. I delivered a beautiful baby boy.

'The gentleman took the child in his arms. He said to me, "It is a relief that you are with us. Will you stay a little while longer, until I know that my wife and son are well? I will pay you in gold."

He took a little jar from the mantelpiece.

"'In my family we have an ailment. Our eyes itch. If you will smear this stuff on my son's eyelids then we all will be able to sleep. Careful with it. It is good for his eyes but not for yours.'

'Every night I did as I was bid. I dabbed the ointment on his eyelids. But one night I was bathing the baby and he splashed water in my eyes. Before I knew what I had done, I rubbed…

'There must have been some of that stuff on my finger! When I opened my eye … well, with my normal eye I saw a room. With the eye I had rubbed I saw a cave. With my normal eye I saw a planked floor covered in rugs. With the other eye the floor was stone and covered in bones and straw. With my normal eye I saw the baby, but with the other eye I saw a creature – beautiful, but not human … utterly other. I looked at the mother. With my normal eye I saw a woman in bed. With the other eye I saw a creature laid in filthy straw, beautiful, but not human. She was as pale as the moon.

'I turned away; I resumed my chores. With one eye I was walking down a corridor, with the other a tunnel. With one eye I saw the wet nurse approaching, with the other … it was your Mari! Her face was streaked with dirt, her clothes ragged, but I knew her.

'She saw me start and whispered, "The Tylwyth Teg took me. They steal human women to feed their children. They left something in my place. The ointment that you rubbed on your eye makes you see the world as it really is, not as they want you to see it. They want you to believe you are among people, but in truth you are among the fairies: the Tylwyth Teg. The ointment has broken their spell. They can never deceive you again. If they find out, you're dead. Tell the creature all is well with mother and child and you need to go home. Tell Matthew that on May Eve all of us, the whole house of us, will travel down the mill road. Tell him he is to wait at the crossroads. As I pass by, tell him to grab me. He must hold on, no matter what he sees. If he does so there is a chance he can free me."

'I found the gentleman of the house. With one eye he was just as he had been when he had come to my door. With the other he was a thin creature, quite beautiful, and pale as the moon.

'"Mother and son are well. If you please, I want to go home now."

'He fetched a sack. "This is to thank you for all you have done for us."

'He led me out into the night. I looked over my shoulder. With one eye I saw the fine house. With the other I saw the Bryn, pocked with caves.

'I went home. I opened the sack on the kitchen table. With one eye I saw golden coins. With the other, dead brown dry leaves.'

The widow Rhys said to Matthew, 'I can see by the look on your face that you don't believe me. But there is a way to test my story. Go to the graveyard. Dig up your wife's coffin. If you find your wife, then I am mad. If you find something else, then I speak truth.'

So it was that the good Christian man Matthew Pritchard found himself in the graveyard at midnight, digging up his wife's grave. He heaped squares of turf beside her plot and dug until his shirt stuck to his back with the sweat. He reached up out of the hole and fetched down a lantern. He saw the coffin lid. He unscrewed the bolts, lifted it... The guts inside his belly twisted. In the coffin was a tree trunk carved in the shape of a woman. The arms were branches, the fingers twigs ... in the wooden head, where the eyes should have been, were two holes, each containing a little white pebble. A gash of a mouth was full of dog's teeth. On the top of the trunk had been fixed bloody matted clumps of Mari's hair. He whispered a prayer, crossed himself, slammed down the lid, tightened the bolts, shovelled on the earth and put the squares of turf back in place in half the time it had taken him to dig them up.

On May eve, Matthew and the widow Rhys walked down the mill road. The old woman glanced over her shoulder now and then. When they reached the crossroads, they stood and waited.

'They are coming, a host of them. When I give the sign, reach out and grab the air in front of you. Don't let go, no matter what happens.'

Pritchard, feeling a fool, waited. He was shaking. She gave the sign. His arms clasped around something he couldn't see. He held it tight, warm and heavy against him. Suddenly the trees were thrashing. Shining creatures were lunging at him, scratching him, but still he held on tight. Then he saw his wife in the arms of the pale creature, laughing at him, mocking him, but still he held on tight. Then he saw his mother, his father, long dead, calling to him, reaching for him, pleading with him to let go and take them instead, but still he held on tight. Then he saw his children, cowering from a cat with the face of a man, but still he held on tight. Then the thing in his arms was a wriggling eel. Then it was a blazing branch. A roaring lion…

And then the trees were still. All was silent. And he held his wife in his arms.

After that, Mari never missed a Sunday at chapel. As for the widow Rhys, one day she was down in the market and saw a thief, his back to her, stealing!

'You! Stop!' she said.

The people around her turned to see who she was speaking to, but they saw no one. The thief turned. The widow Rhys put her hand over one eye then the other. She only saw him with one eye, the one she had smeared with the ointment. It was the pale, beautiful creature from the cave, the father of the child.

'I told you not to use that stuff. Which eye do you see me with?'

She pointed.

'This eye has seen too much,' he said. He blew on it. She blinked. When she opened her eye, she could see nothing through it. And she never saw anything from it again, nothing from this world or the other. But always she knew that the Tylwyth Teg walked among us, unseen, watching.

SPELLBOUND

A queen ruled a nation long ago. She gave birth to a son. One night the queen dreamed that if her son's feet touched the ground before he was twelve years old, he would be spellbound. So as an infant he was carried by his nurse; as he grew older, he drove a carriage, with a servant to lift him up and down. When he was a little older still, he rode a horse; the servant lifted him onto the horse when he set out and lifted him off the horse when he came home. The queen loved him so much. At night she would creep from her bedchamber, open his bedroom door, and watch her beautiful boy sleeping.

The day before the prince's twelfth birthday, the queen prepared a great feast to give thanks.

'Tomorrow, you will walk and run and play in the garden like every other child!' she said.

The next morning, the groom fetched the prince's horse for him to go riding; and the servant carried the prince out into the courtyard to lift him onto the horse's back.

The prince has one foot in the stirrup,
he waves to the queen watching from a window,
he is laughing to think how tomorrow he will be free.
The sky grows dark,
there is a clap of thunder,
the earth trembles,
the horse rears,
the servant lets go,
the young prince falls from the horse's back...
Darkness!
The prince has gone.
Vanished!

The queen wept. Everyone in the palace was frantic, searching, searching, searching. All in vain. The whole country was scoured, a reward offered for the finding of the prince.

All in vain.

The prince's bedroom was kept just as it had been when he had left it. Years passed. On the night of what would have been his eighteenth birthday, a servant was passing the prince's bedroom when she heard moaning and whispering. The servant opened the door to see no one. Moonlight was shining through the window on to the bed. But the room was full of strange sounds.

The servant fetched the queen. The next midnight they went to the room. And so it went on, midnight after midnight. Word spread that the room was haunted.

The queen dreamt again. This time she heard a voice.

The voice said, 'Your son is spellbound. If the right woman – but not you – stayed in the room all night, it may be that she could break the spell.'

The queen offered three hundred pieces of gold to any woman who would stay in the haunted room the whole night.

Times were hard. Many different women answered the call, but always at midnight there came such dreadful sounds they took fright and fled. Three hundred pieces of gold weren't enough to make them stay.

Not far away from the palace there lived a widow with three daughters. She owned a little mill, and by grinding corn for the neighbours she just managed to make a living. But it wasn't much of a life.

The eldest daughter told her mother, 'For three hundred gold pieces I would kiss a donkey's behind! I will go to the palace.'

'Good!' said the mother. 'Go, and good luck to you!'

So, the eldest daughter went to the queen. She asked for food to cook her supper and dry wood to light a fire, a cooking pot and a lantern. She promised the queen that she wouldn't come out of the room until morning.

She made the bed, lit the fire, put the food in the cooking pot, then the cooking pot on the fire and waited.

At midnight, when the food was ready, she heard the strangest sound!

'Who is it? Show yourself!'

She peered behind the curtain at no one. She dropped to her hands and knees and peered under the bed. When she straightened up again, the prince was standing over her. His eyes were wide. He was frail and pale. He looked so tired.

He said, 'For whom are you cooking?'

She answered, 'Me.'

'For whom is the table spread?'

'Me.'

'For whom is the bed made?'

'Me.'

The prince's shoulders shook. Tears ran down his cheeks. He sobbed.

'It is so long since I have eaten! So long since I have slept!'

One moment he was there, wretched with despair, then he was gone.

She ate her supper and went to bed.

Next morning, when she told the queen what had happened, the queen said, 'You are not the one.'

But a promise is a promise. The queen gave her three hundred gold pieces.

When the second daughter saw the gold she said to her mother, 'Me next!'

And it all came about just as it had done with her older sister.

'For whom are you cooking?' the young man asked again.

'Me,' the second daughter said.

'For whom is the table spread?'

'Me.'

'For whom is the bed made?'

'Me.'

'It is so long since I have eaten! So long since I have slept!'

The prince sobbed, his shoulders shook, then he was gone.

Next morning, she went to the queen and asked for her three hundred gold pieces.

The queen sighed and handed them over.

'You are not the one either.'

When the second daughter returned to her family, the youngest daughter said, 'I will try.'

'Yes!' said the other sisters. 'You go and get your three hundred gold pieces!'

'I want to free him!'

'Don't be so selfish!' said the eldest sister. 'As long as he is spellbound, there's gold to be had!'

'I know he is a prince, but he is also a human being in torment. To be so alone! To feel so much despair that you weep every night!'

She went to the palace. The queen sighed, but she agreed to supply the things the young woman asked for: a lantern, sticks to light a fire, food for her supper, and a cooking pot. In the room, the youngest daughter put the pot on the fire, put the food in the pot, made the bed and waited.

At midnight came the footsteps, the sighs, the groans. The girl's heart pounded, but she held her nerve. In a blink, in a moment, he appeared. How sad and weary he looked!

'For whom are you cooking?' the prince asked.

'What is mine is yours,' said the youngest daughter.

'For whom is the table laid?'

'What is mine is yours.'

'For whom is the bed made?'

'What is mine is yours.'

'Thank you from my heart. Before I sup, and sleep, I must thank the others who have been kind to me.'

Then the woman felt a sweet soft breeze on her

cheek, she smelled blossom, and the floor under her was gone. The prince was descending slowly into darkness. She followed him, not walking but drifting down and down. It was dark and strange, but she didn't turn back.

She was in another world. A river flowed with liquid gold. In the distance could be seen the crests of golden mountains. In between the river and the mountains was a meadow bright with flowers. The prince walked. She followed. He didn't turn to look at her. He didn't seem to know she was there.

He knelt.

'Thank you, flowers. Your beauty gave me hope when I had none.'

The flowers bowed their heads.

He came to a forest of golden trees with birds on every branch.

'Thank you. Without your music I would have lost heart.'

As she passed through the forest, she picked up a golden branch.

They came to a forest of silver. Animals gathered at his feet.

'Thank you. Without your company I would surely have succumbed to despair. Farewell.'

She took a silver branch. Back they went through the golden forest of birds.

'Farewell.'

Across the meadow of flowers.

'Farewell. I will always remember your kindness.'

Now the prince rose up. The youngest daughter rose up behind him, until they were back in the bedroom. For the first time he smiled.

'Now I can eat.'

They ate.

'At last,' he said. 'I can sleep.'

And he laid down on the bed and slept. She lay and drifted into slumber beside him.

Next morning, the queen waited impatiently for the young woman to emerge from her son's chamber. By midday she could wait no longer. She made her way to the bedroom, pushed open the door...

In the bed there was a young woman, and another ... a beautiful young man with a golden branch at his head and a silver branch at his feet.

THE TALE OF
DANIEL CROWLEY

In the great Irish city of Cork there lived a man named Daniel Crowley. He was a coffin maker, and business was good. He had a workshop, a home above it, and three apprentices working for him. His work was his whole life. He lived alone. He wasn't much for talk. He'd look at people gathered on the street and wonder how they could think of so much to say day after day.

At six o'clock one winter's night, a message came. A gentleman had breathed his last, and would Daniel send a coffin at once? Daniel did nothing much of an evening, so rather than send an apprentice, he thought he would deliver it himself. He loaded a coffin on the cart, pulled down the shutters on the shop windows and locked the door. He climbed on the cart, shook the reins and his donkey set off.

Daniel wound his way slowly through the streets. There was no hurry. The dead man wasn't going anywhere.

In Ireland, the night before a funeral, they have a gathering in honour of the person who has died, to wish them farewell. It is called a wake. When Daniel reached the gentleman's house, the wake was in full swing. He heard music and laughter. Some of the guests were even dancing. The corpse was laid out on a table in the front room. Five or six women were keeping watch around it, but most of the guests were making merry in the kitchen. Daniel was never comfortable at such gatherings. He wanted to do his business and be off, but the family of the gentleman wouldn't hear of that. It was their duty to make him welcome. They peeled off his coat, plucked his hat from his head, pushed a glass of whiskey into his hand – and then another, and another.

Among the guests a mother turned to her friend and pointed. 'There's that Daniel Crowley. He's rich, lives alone, and here I am with three unmarried daughters at home! He wants a wife to share his life! It would be the making of him. Go and see if you can talk some sense into him.'

The friend went to Crowley and said, 'Isn't it time for you to think of settling down? There's a woman here who has three beautiful daughters...'

'I am settled down, thank you. There isn't a woman alive that I would marry.'

The mother heard this and said, 'What a thing to say! It is as if you prefer the company of the dead than the living!'

'I do! The living are always fussing about something! Arguing, fretting ... you don't hear the dead complaining!'

'Why don't you have a party with them then?'

'If I could, I would.' He'd had a few glasses of whiskey, so he stepped forward, hushed the crowd, and cried, 'Hear me now! Men, women, children, soldiers, sailors, all the people that I have ever made coffins for, I invite you tonight to my home!' He bowed to the mother, retrieved his coat and hat and was gone into the night.

When he had gone, in the front room, a woman gasped.

'Look!'

The corpse on the table was smiling…

Meanwhile Crowley made his way through the dark, sleeping streets. He didn't see another soul – until he turned the corner of the road where he lived. When he had set off he had locked his shop, but light was streaming from the windows and the doorway, and he heard laughter and singing from inside. Crowley jumped down from his cart. He crept into a corner and watched the dark shapes of men, women and children entering his shop. Then he felt a hand on his shoulder, and someone said, 'Why are you out here? We're all waiting for you!'

Crowley turned to see a pale man who said, 'Don't you recognise me?'

'Sorry. Should I?'

'Ah! Forgive me. You meet so many people in your line of work. I am the first man you ever made a coffin for. Come and meet everyone!'

They stepped out of the corner into the light of a streetlamp. The man didn't look at all well. His skin was saggy and grey and there was a hole in his cheek.

They went into the shop. The guests were all corpses! And they'd found his secret stash of whiskey. The dead hugged him and shook his hand. Oh, the smell! He gagged and said to his new friend, 'How can I get rid of them?'

'But the party's just started. It's only 2 am!'

Crowley said, 'See that woman, sitting alone? She won't meet my eye.'

'She's embarrassed. Her family still owe you for her coffin. She's afraid you are going to demand the rest of the money in front of everyone.'

John Healy was there, the famous fiddler, but of course he had left his fiddle behind when he'd gone into the ground, so he had nothing to play. He pulled some long strands of hair from a passing woman's head, strapped them to a stray leg bone, peeled the skin off his chest and began scraping his ribs. At the sound of the music the whole company threw off their flesh and danced jigs in their bare bones. One man was blowing into his stomach lining as if it was bagpipes. A woman was whacking her skull with a pair of chisels for percussion.

Daniel stood amidst them all, appalled.

One man, Sullivan, had a problem. When his first wife died, he had married again, and Crowley had supplied the coffins for both wives! Sullivan danced with the second wife so well that all the skeletons cheered – except his first wife, who cried, 'Get off her!'

But the second wife said, 'Be fair. You were dead and gone by the time he took up with me!'

The first wife said, 'Sullivan, those aren't her legs.'

Sullivan stopped dancing and looked down.

'I borrowed them,' said the second wife.

'Whose legs are they?' asked Sullivan.

'Catherine Murray's.'

'Catherine Murray's?'

'I seem to remember you liking her legs when you were alive!'

'Why didn't you bring your own?'

'I always had two left feet and Catherine was an excellent dancer.'

The first wife said, 'You don't know where those legs have been.'

'Never judge a person till you have walked a week on her legs!' answered the second wife.

The first wife walloped the second. The second hit back. The families of both wives joined in. They pulled off their left arms and swung them about in a terrible fashion. Daniel Crowley dodged and ducked and shielded his head. Sullivan stumbled into Daniel and trod on his toe; Daniel punched him so hard the head came off his corpse and flew across the room. Sullivan barged through the melee, grabbed his head and threw it back. It struck Daniel. He tumbled under a bench and Sullivan jumped on him. The last thing Daniel remembered was Sullivan's cold, bony fingers around his throat...

Such a mess the apprentices found in the morning! Broken windows and bottles; tools everywhere, tables and chairs turned upside down ... and amidst it all, Crowley lay unconscious, his neck purple.

As soon as he was able to, Daniel Crowley travelled to the house of the mother of three daughters. He took off his hat and offered her a bunch of flowers.

'I hope you can forgive my rudeness. If you would still consider me for your son-in-law, I would like to meet with one of your lovely daughters – whichever likes me the most.

Last night I discovered the dead are the same as the living.'

THE
BOY WHO
KEPT A
SECRET

THE BOY WHO KEPT A SECRET

9

Once upon a time a poor widow struggled to feed her four strong sons. Though the lads were identical on the outside, they were very different on the inside. The first three were restless for adventure. The youngest was a dreamer, never happier than when he was alone in the countryside.

One summer afternoon, as he worked in a farmer's field, the youngest son saw through the heat haze an old woman approaching. She staggered so much that she went from one side of the path to the other as much that as she moved forwards. He filled a bottle with cold water from the stream and took it to her. As she lifted the bottle to her lips, he heard a clink. She smiled and to his dismay he saw her teeth were made of iron! Iron teeth meant she was a Jezibaba, a spirit who walks the world in the guise of an old woman. They either give a gift or take your life.

'Thank you for your kindness,' she said. 'What is your name?'

'Janos.'

'What are you? Boy or man?'

'A boy.'

'Well, boy, would you like a toy?'

She gave Janos a scabbard – a sheath for a sword.

'See you next time,' she said. And she went on her way.

The scabbard was beautiful, carved with curling, swirling patterns. Janos strapped it to his belt and marched about the field.

'I am a soldier now!'

When he went home at the end of the day, his brothers said, 'What is that?'

'A scabbard, a sheath for a sword.'

'Throw it away. You have nothing to put in it.'

'You know how it goes. If I throw the scabbard away, then the very next day I will find a sword!'

His brothers sneered and tapped the sides of their heads.

"Your scabbard ain't got no sword!'

'Your broom ain't got no brushes!'

'There's a hole in your bucket!'

Janos ignored them. Even though they teased him, he wore his scabbard every day; it was beautiful and it belonged to him. It wasn't a hand-me-down like everything else he had – even his shoes had belonged to his brothers.

Janos was at the age when you could almost see him growing. He was shooting up like a sapling. And a strange thing was, as he grew, so did the scabbard. His brothers were jealous of it. They teased him so cruelly that one evening, in tears, he slipped into the garden to bury it. As he scooped apart the earth between the strawberry plants, he saw something shining in the dirt. It was a sword! Mindful of his brothers, he covered it up.

On the morning of his birthday, as he sat at the table eating breakfast, he threw back his head and laughed.

'What is funny?' asked his mother.

He froze.

'Nothing.'

'It must be something! What?'

'I had a dream last night, that's all.'

'Huh!' said one of his brothers. 'Dreams!'

'What was the dream?' his mother asked.

'I'm not telling.'

'Why not?'

'If I tell you, it won't come true.'

'If you can't tell me, who can you tell?'

'No one. I can tell no one.'

'Listen to you! You weren't abandoned on the doorstep by the royal family. You are my son. I know because I was there when you were born! I have a right to know your dreams! After all I have done for you, can you not do this little thing for me?'

'I won't.'

'That is because there was no dream! You were laughing at *us!* You sit there, sneering, smirking, judging. You think you are better than the rest of us. Get out! Out!'

She pushed him through the front door. He fell on the path. As he lay there, he heard a strange sound. The sword was spinning above the strawberry patch. As soon as he touched it, it stopped. He held it in his hand... It fitted the scabbard!

The door behind him opened.

His mother said, 'All I ask is that you talk to me

once in a while, so that I have some idea of what is going on in your head, but no, I am not worthy!' And she slammed the door.

Janos' lip began to tremble. His eyes prickled. Just then, a carriage passed by. A rich man looked out.

'What is the matter? Why are you crying?'

'My mother threw me out.'

'You could work for me ... I could do with someone like you!'

'Yes! Thank you.'

'Coachman! Stop!'

The rich man knocked on the door of the house. Janos' mother opened it. He said, 'Can your son come to live and work for me?'

'I hope you have more luck with him than I do!' she said. She slammed the door again.

As they travelled in the carriage, the rich man said: 'So why did your mother throw you out?'

'Because I wouldn't tell her my dream.'

'Why wouldn't you tell her?'

'Because if I tell anyone it won't come true.'

'Would you tell me?'

Janos shook his head.

'I know who you will tell … one of my three daughters!'

When they reached the rich man's house he called, 'Daughters! I have a surprise!'

The daughters liked the look of Janos. He was a strong young man, broad and tall and rough-skinned.

'He keeps a secret,' said the rich man. 'A dream. He won't speak of it.'

'Tell me…' said the eldest.

'I can't,' replied Janos.

'Tell me!' said the second sister.

'I can't,' he answered.

He thought the youngest the loveliest of the three…

'Surely you will tell me?' she said.

'I cannot! Please don't ask me again!'

'Oh, how disappointing,' said the rich man. 'I was hoping you might become my son-in-law, but if that is the way you want to play it, off you go to the servants' quarters.'

Janos didn't mind. He was used to work, and he was away from his cruel brothers. Years went by. Janos grew. The sword and the scabbard grew too. On his seventeenth birthday Janos was digging the garden when the youngest daughter chanced upon him.

'Who are you?'

'Janos.'

'Ah! I remember. You are the one with the secret. Tell it to me.'

'I can't.'

'Just me...'

'I am sorry!'

'If you tell it to me, I will marry you.'

'I can't. Please don't ask me again.'

She scowled. 'Tell me!'

She pushed him. He pushed her back. She fell, burst into tears, ran to her father and showed him her muddy dress.

'Look what Janos did!'

'This is how he repays my kindness. I brought a cuckoo into the nest! Before he does any more harm, I will have him slung in jail.'

Janos was taken to town, tried and sentenced to hang. A gallows was built in the market square. The people gathered to see the young man who had dared to lay his hand on the rich man's daughter. Janos was led out by the executioner. He made his way through the crowd to the foot of the gallows. Just as he was about to lift his foot onto the first step, into the square rolled the king's carriage. The king leaned out.

'I say! Why are you hanging that handsome lad?'

'He hurt a rich man's daughter.'

'Why did you hurt her?'

'She hurt me.'

'Why did she hurt you?'

'Because I wouldn't tell her my dream.'

'I know who you will tell – my daughter! Untie him. Come with me!'

It so happened that when Janos arrived, the king's daughter was picking flowers in the garden. Janos thought her as beautiful as the morning star. When she saw him, she dropped the flowers and ran to her father.

'Who is this vision of beauty? Did you find him in fairyland?'

'No, at the foot of the gallows.'

'I don't care where you found him. I want him for my husband.'

'Do you know why he was about to be hanged? For hurting a rich man's daughter.'

She said to Janos, 'Why did you hurt a rich man's daughter?'

'Because she hurt me.'

'Why did she hurt you?'

'Because I wouldn't tell her my dream.'

'Good! I love a challenge!'

A few days later, Janos was digging in the garden when the king's daughter came to him. He thought her so beautiful, the sword in his scabbard rattled.

'Whisper your secret in my ear and I will give you a kiss,' she said.

'I can't.'

The princess always got what she wanted.

'Why not?'

'Because if I tell anyone, it won't come true.'

'TELL ME!'

She pushed him. He pushed her back. She fell into the mud. She ran. When the king saw the dirt on her dress, he said, 'How dare he lay a hand on you! Seize him! And send for the builders!

'You, build me a tower at once.'

The masons set to work. When it was ready, the guards shoved Janos into the tower and bricked up the gap behind him.

'You will starve to death for your insolence!' the king said.

But as soon as her father had gone, the princess said, 'Mason, wait.'

At her instruction, he made a secret gap, a hole on the wall, through which the princess pushed food and water.

'You were foolish – but so was I,' she said to Janos. 'I won't let a man die for the sake of two foolish moments.'

Every day the king would go to the tower.

'Janos! Are you dead yet?'

Every day the same reply...

'Not yet, Your Majesty.'

How odd, the king thought. *There is magic in this.*

But soon the king had cause to forget Janos. A gift arrived from the Sultan of Turkey. The king opened it and found three sticks. The messenger bowed.

'My master told me to tell you, these pieces of cane were cut from the same bamboo. If you are clever enough to be a king, you will know which piece grew from nearest the root, which from the middle and which from the top. If you do not know, then you are not fit to rule, and the Sultan will take your kingdom. You have a week.'

The king turned the shoots over in his hand. They were identical. Next day, the princess saw her father looking glum. He told her of the message, then he said, 'My army is small. His is vast.'

That evening when the princess took food to the tower, Janos said, 'Something is wrong. What is the matter?'

She told him. He replied, 'Go to bed tonight and rest easy. Tomorrow, this is what you must do...'

Next morning, she ran in her nightdress to her father's bedchamber.

'Father, I have had such a dream! Servants, fetch a bucket of warm water.'

She dropped the three canes into the bucket. One sank, one bobbed up and down, and the other floated.

'It is just as the dream foretold. Send for the messenger. This is what you must tell him...'

When the messenger came, the king said, 'Dry wood sinks but fresh floats. The shoot that sank is from the top of the stalk. The shoot that bobs up and down is from the middle. The shoot that floats on the surface is from the bottom of the stem.'

The messenger bowed and set off without a word. When he relayed the news, standing behind the sultan's throne was an old woman with iron teeth – another Jezibaba like one Janos had met by the river!

'Someone told him the answer,' she said. 'No king alive knows the simple things of the world. How would he know what kinds of wood floats? Who told him? Your Excellency, this is what you must do...'

The messenger returned to the King of Hungary with three foals. He bowed.

'Your Highness, his Excellency the Sultan is concerned for your people. If a ruler is a fool, then his subjects suffer. Which of these foals was born first, which second and which last? If you do not know then you will have shown the world you are not wise enough to sit on the throne and the sultan will take your crown. You have a week.' He bowed again.

The horses were identical.

The daughter found her father staring at the floor. He told his story. She ran to the tower. Janos listened and said,

'This is what you must do.'

Next morning, the king came to her bed-chamber.

'Dream anything useful?'

'I dreamed that Janos has the answer.'

'Servants! Pull down the tower! Bring me Janos!'

Janos came. 'Your Highness,' he said, 'send for three troughs. Into the first put oats, the second, wheat and the third, barley.'

The troughs were fetched. The foals were brought. Each went to a different trough.

'The horse who chose the oats is the oldest because she knows the most. She knows oats will give her strength. The one who ate the cheap corn was born second. The one who chose the barley knows nothing yet, because she does not know what is good for her to eat, so she is the youngest.'

The king relayed the answer to the messenger.

When the messenger took the answer to the sultan's court, the Jezibaba said, 'Kings don't know one end of a trough from the other, let alone what foals like to eat. Servants feed their horses. Someone is helping the king, a rough peasant with dirt under his fingernails. If you want Hungary, you must get rid of him.'

The messenger returned to the king.

'Your Highness, the sultan says you are too stupid to have solved these riddles. You are to send the peasant who answered them. If you do not, the sultan will come with an army, and take your land. And be warned. There are as many soldiers in his army as there are stars in a summer sky.'

The king took Janos to one side.

'I am sorry. What can I do? It is one life for the sake of many.'

'Your Highness, this is what you must do…'

Janos' brothers were summoned and went with him to Turkey. The four identical brothers stood before the sultan. The messenger was shaking as he said, 'Your Excellency, the King of Hungary says, "We have solved your riddles, now it is your turn to solve ours. Which of these young men is the one you seek? If you cannot tell, then you are not fit to rule Turkey, let alone Hungary, and His Highness will send storytellers all over the world to tell tales of your stupidity until the mere mention of your name will bring forth a smile on the lips of every man, woman and child on the planet. You have a week.'

The Jezibaba whispered to the sultan, 'Leave this to me.'

That night she made herself invisible and crept into the brothers' bedchamber. She watched.

'Did you see the woman behind the throne?' Janos asked his brothers. 'The one with the iron teeth? She is a Jezibaba. She is the one who set these riddles. The sultan is too stupid to have done so.'

When the brothers slept, she silently cut a button from Janos' shirt.

Next morning, as they dressed, Janos noticed the missing button... He said, 'This is what we will do...'

They were summoned to the throne room.

'I,' said the sultan, 'am more than a match for your king. The one who is missing a button step forward.'

They all took a step. The sultan saw they were all missing a button. The Jezibaba ground together her iron teeth. That night as he slept, she cut a lock from Janos' hair.

Next morning all of the brothers were missing hair from the same part of their heads.

'Kill them all!'

Janos' sword flew from the scabbard and ... shik, shik! Seven guards fell to the floor. The sultan stared aghast at the carnage before him. He turned to his Jezibaba.

'You told me that with your help I would win the land of Hungary with no bloodshed. Look! seven sons of Turkey lie dead! Seven mothers will weep tonight. Seven fathers will soak their pillows with hot tears! I want no more of this.'

Meanwhile in Hungary, the princess was anxious. The days slipped by, and Janos did not return. She dressed herself in her father's armour and led his army to the border between Turkey and Hungary. When she saw Janos and his brothers returning safely, she shouted for joy. They went back to her father's palace.

'The sultan was right,' said the king. 'I am too stupid to wear the crown. You are better fit to rule Hungary than I am. Marry my daughter and take the throne.'

Janos put the crown on his head.

'Send for my mother, the rich man and his daughter,' he asked.

Before them all he said, 'Now I can tell you my secret. I dreamed I would become the King of Hungary. But mother, if I had told you my dream, you would not have thrown me out. If you had not thrown me out, I wouldn't have gone with the rich man. If I hadn't gone with the rich man, I wouldn't have been sent to the gallows. If I hadn't been sent to the gallows, the king wouldn't have seen me. If the king hadn't seen me, he wouldn't have taken me to his palace, his daughter wouldn't have fallen in love with me, and I would never have become king. That is why I did not tell you my dream.'

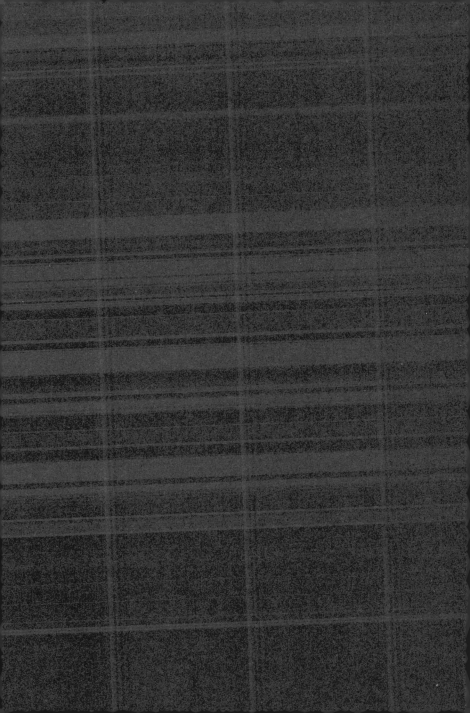